FOR
Theodor & Alfred

Anne-Kathrin Behl grew up as the daughter of a bookseller and a forester in Greifswald, Germany. She studied illustration at the Hamburg University of Applied Sciences (HAW) in Hamburg and now lives with her husband and two sons in Leipzig, where she works as a freelance illustrator and writer for various publishers. Her books have been translated into many languages and awarded the Prix Chronos de Littérature. They've also been included in the collection of the most beautiful children's books as part of the Austrian Children's and Young Adult Literature Prize.

First published in the United States, Great Britain, Canada, Australia, and New Zealand in 2020 by NorthSouth Books, Inc., an imprint of NordSüd Verlag AG, CH-8050 Zürich, Switzerland.

Distributed in the United States by NorthSouth Books, Inc., New York 10016.
Library of Congress Cataloging-in-Publication Data is available.

ISBN: 978-0-7358-4431-5
Printed in Livonia Print, Riga, Latvia
1 3 5 7 9 • 10 8 6 4 2
www.northsouth.com

ANNE-KATHRIN BEHL

Robert
AND THE WORLD'S BEST
CAKE

Translated by David Henry Wilson

North
South

Robert and his father had the day off. They spent the morning on the sunlit balcony. Robert had an idea. "I'll bake a cake! A gigantic cake! You're invited to have some cake, Dad, and so are ALL my cuddly toys and of course Mopsi too."

Nothing ever happened without Robert's dog, Mopsi.

"First of all, we should write some invitations. That's what people do when there's a big cake party," Robert explained.

Robert found some paper and his favorite colored pencils. He imagined exactly how the cake would look.

The invitations were ready.

GREAT
CAKE PARTY
3PM
at Robert's house

But just as Robert put the invitations down on the table, there was a big gust of wind. All the cards flew away.

"Oh no!" cried Robert, and sadly watched the invitations disappear.

But then Robert discovered that two of the cards were still lying on the table.

"This one's for you, Dad. And the other is for Mopsi."

Next, Robert prepared everything for the big bake. Of course he needed to have a clean and tidy work surface for the batter. This meant he had to move some of his toys out of the way.

Dad mixed the batter and Robert piled it up into a great heap.

"We need more batter!" Robert called out to the kitchen, because he knew that a big dad needs a big cake.

"And some more!"
Dad had to make batter five more times. Then at last the cake was big enough.

Robert searched his room for everything that was needed to finish the cake. *Model cars and puzzle pieces will make good decorations for the topping…*

...and pencils will do very nicely instead of candles.

IT'S ALL READY!

Dad dressed up for the cake party. He reached out for the first piece, but suddenly the doorbell rang.

Robert's friend Lea was standing at the door.
"Hi, Robert!" she said. She was holding an invitation in her hand.
"I found this in the street. Please, can I have a piece of cake?"
"Yes!" cried Robert. "Come on in!"

The doorbell rang again.
"Hello, Robert!" said his friends Emma and Oscar at the same time. "These invitations are from you, aren't they? Please, can we join you?"
"Yes!" cried Robert. "Come on in!"

Then the doorbell rang again....

"Are you Robert's father?" asked a policewoman.

"Y-yes," stammered Robert's dad.

"I just found this card. Please, can I have a piece of cake too?"

"Yes!" cried Robert's dad. "Come on in!"

Now the doorbell rang again...

...and again.

Soon the hall was full. There was no room for anyone else.

Robert squeezed through the crowd and looked at his cake.
Suddenly it seemed extremely small.
He looked back at all the guests.
"I think we need…

MORE CAKE !